Un fortunately

Alan Durant

ORCHARD BOOKS

Simon Rickerty

One bright, sunny day, a boy was walking happily through the jungle, whistling.

Unfortunately, he met a big, scary lion with very sharp teeth.

The lion ROARED and leapt at the boy.

Fortunately, the boy quickly climbed up a tree and escaped.

... a mean and hungry snake was coiled around the tree.

It opened its mouth to swallow the boy.

"Uh-oh!"

Fortunately, the boy grabbed a vine . . .

. . . and swung away from the snake.

"WHEE!"

Unfortunately, the vine broke and the boy . . . .

. . . dropped into a mire of quicksand.

"HELP!"

Fortunately, a hunter was passing by.

He threw a rope around the boy and hauled him out of the quicksand.

Then, the hunter took the boy back to his village for dinner.

Unfortunately, the boy WAS dinner.

"HELP AGAIN!"

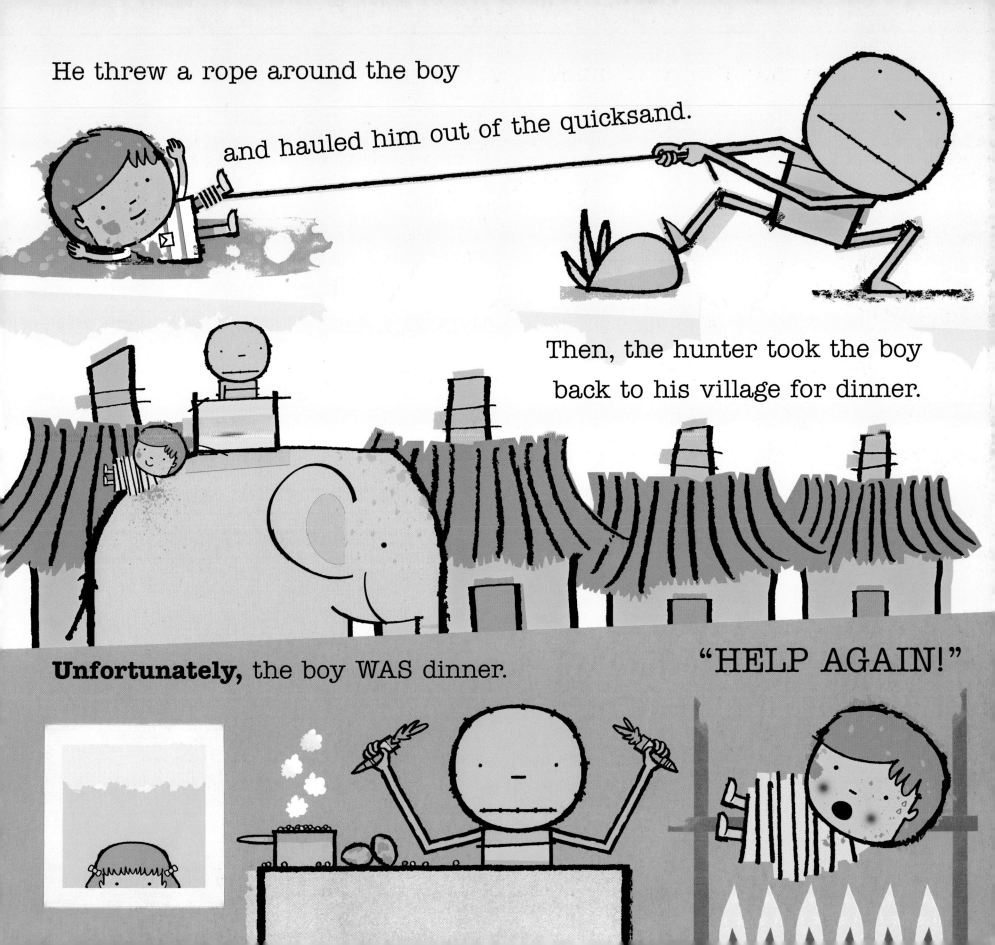

Fortunately, a girl took pity on the boy . . .

. . . and set him free.

They ran away together, back into the jungle.

Unfortunately, they didn't watch
where they were going . . .

. . . and
fell
into
a
deep
pit . . .

. . . in which lived a very fierce man-eating bear.

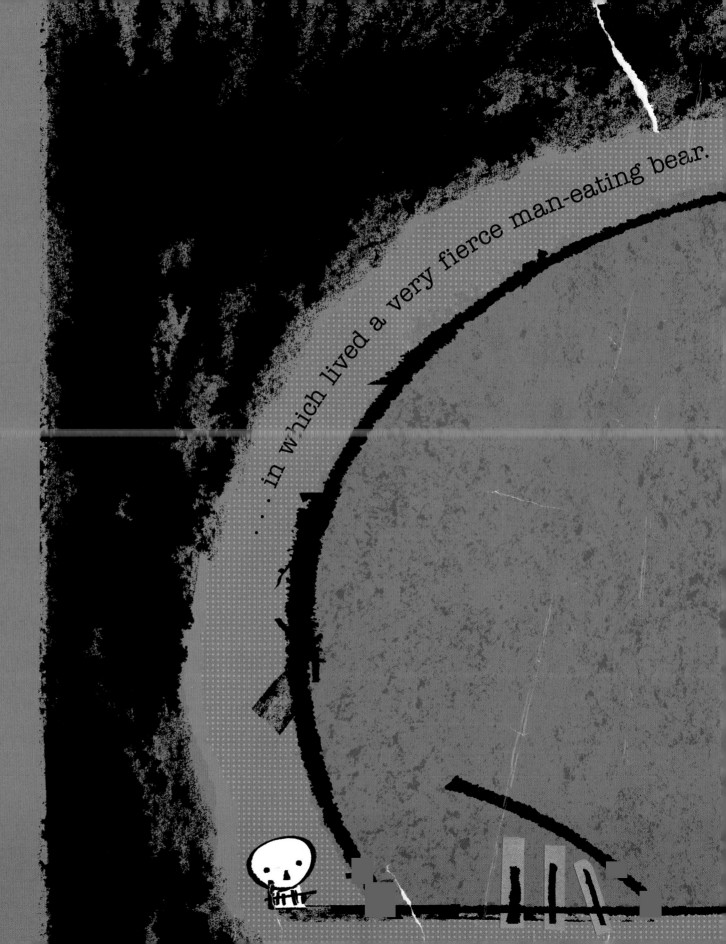

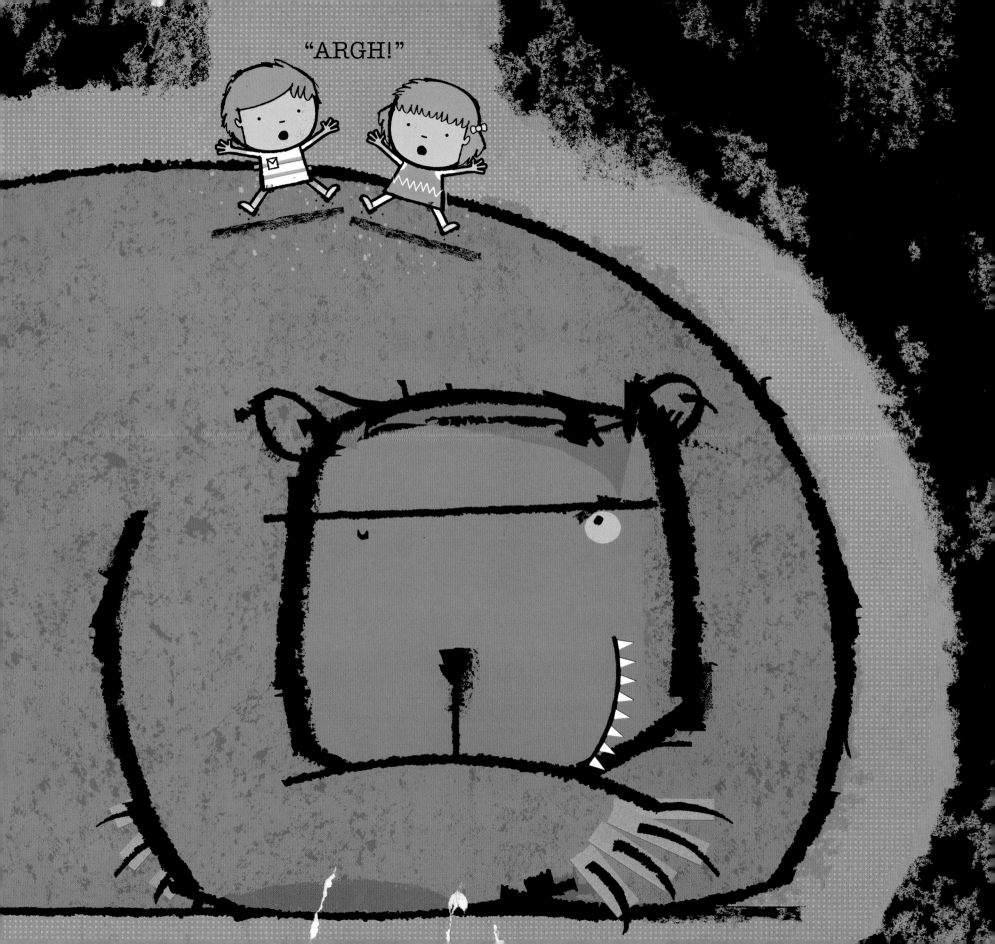

The bear SNARLED and raised its huge paws.

Fortunately, the boy and girl saw a giant web.

"We can climb up this web and escape!" said the boy.

"Good idea," said the girl.

Unfortunately, a giant, venomous, hairy spider appeared . . .

. . . and started to climb down the web towards them.

Closer and closer it came . . .

Fortunately, the boy found a biscuit in his pocket.

He threw it into the web and the spider ate that instead.

The
boy
and
girl
climbed
up
the
web . . .

. . . and
out
of the
pit.

"Free at last!"
they cried.

Unfortunately, a massive vulture flew down . . .

. . . and snatched them up in its talons.

Up it soared, into the sky.

Fortunately, the boy and girl
were too heavy for the vulture
and it dropped them . . .

. . . into a pool.
SPLASH!

Unfortunately,
it was inhabited
by crocodiles.

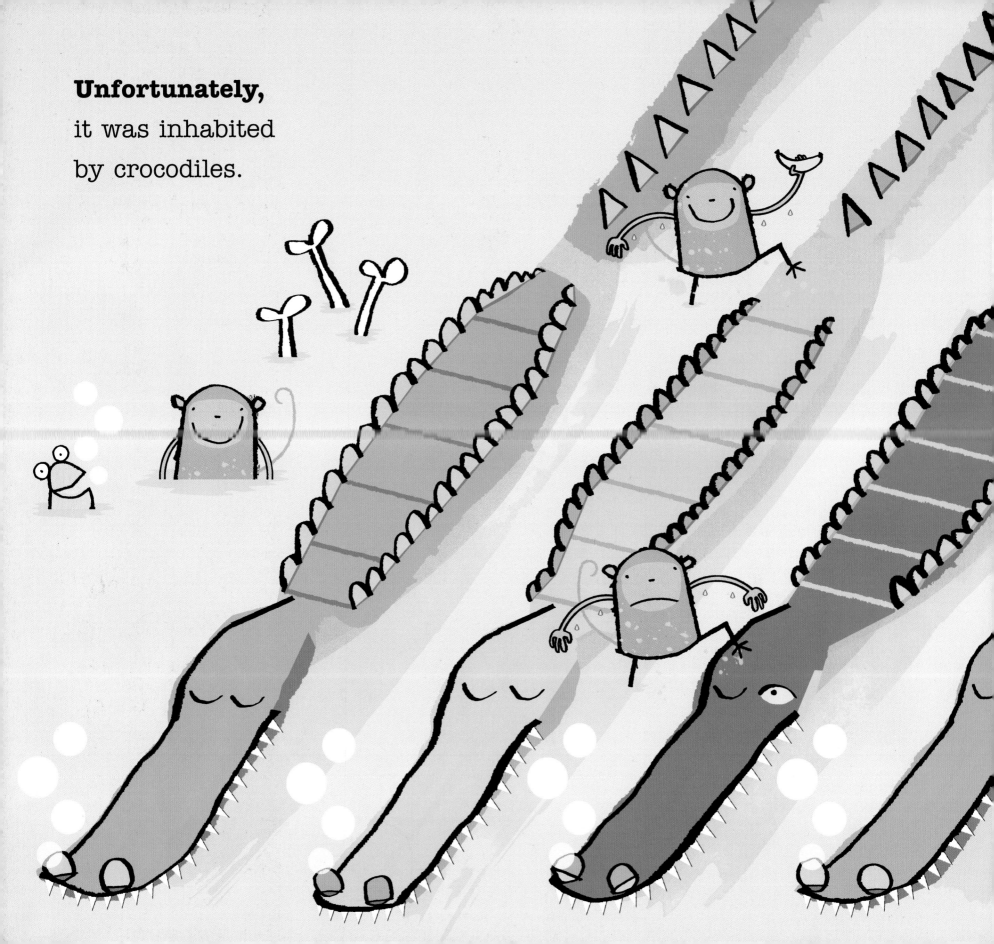

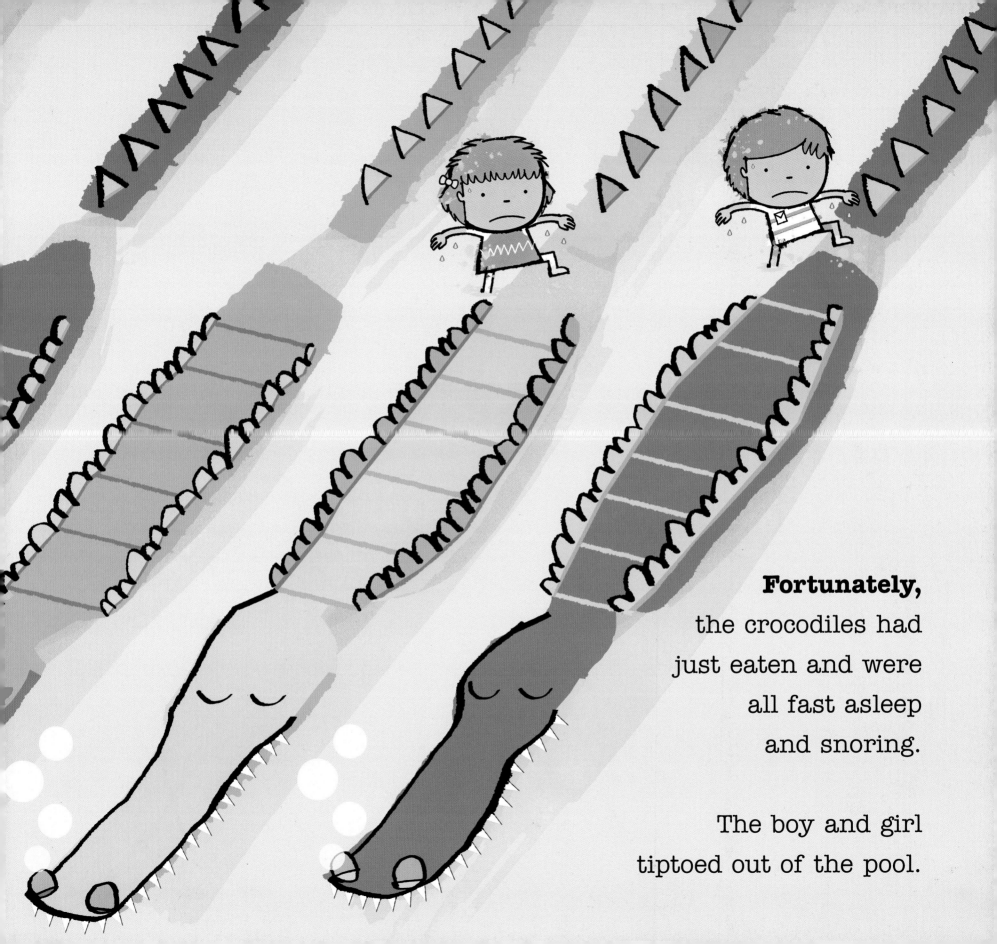

Fortunately, the crocodiles had just eaten and were all fast asleep and snoring.

The boy and girl tiptoed out of the pool.

Then, they walked together happily
through the jungle, whistling . . .